SOMETHING
SPECIAL

SOMETHING
SPECIAL

by David McPhail

HARCOURT BRACE & COMPANY

Orlando Atlanta Austin Boston San Francisco Chicago Dallas New York
Toronto London

The author wishes to thank John O'Connor
for his invaluable assistance

For Damon,
who is something special indeed

This edition is published by special arrangement with
Little, Brown and Company.

Grateful acknowledgment is made to Little, Brown and
Company (Inc.), in association with Joy Street Books for
permission to reprint *Something Special* by David McPhail.
Copyright © 1988 by David McPhail.

Printed in the United States of America
ISBN 0-15-305745-9

1 2 3 4 5 6 7 8 9 10   059   97   96   95   94

Everyone in Sam's family could do something special.
Everyone but Sam.

Sam's sister Sarah played the piano.
Sam loved to watch her fingers fly over the keys.

But when Sam sat down to play it wasn't the same.
"You must have stone fingers, Sam!" Sarah cried.

Sam's sister Flo played first base.
She hardly ever missed a catch.

Sam could watch her play for hours.

Sam wanted to play baseball, too, but he couldn't catch a thing.

"Butterfingers!" said Flo.

Sam's brother, Eugene, was a computer whiz.
He really knew how to make that computer hum.

"Let me try," begged Sam.

But when Sam touched the computer it screamed!

And so did Eugene.

Sam's father was a wonderful cook.
Not only did everything taste good, it looked
beautiful, too.

Once Sam helped cook dinner, but no one
was hungry.

Sam's mother carved wooden birds.
Sam thought they almost looked alive.
He wished he could carve birds, too, but he was
too young to use a sharp knife.

"Maybe Grandma will teach me to knit,"
thought Sam.
"She makes it look so easy."

But it wasn't.

The magician on T.V. made the disappearing
egg trick look easy, too.

But the trick didn't work for Sam, no matter how many times he tried it.

Even Sam's dog, Fred, could do something special.

"I can do *that!*" Sam said.

But he couldn't.

"What else can I try?" Sam wondered.
He walked down to the pond to see the ducks.
The birds were singing.

"Maybe I can sing!" he thought.
But not even the birds would listen.

Sam went to talk to his mother.
She was trying to paint a duck's feathers.
"I just can't get it right," she complained.

"Maybe it should be greener," said Sam,
"like the ducks in the pond."
"Show me," said Mother.

"Why, that's perfect!" Mother said.
"This is fun!" Sam said. "May I paint a picture?"

"That apple looks good enough to eat,"
said his father.

Next Sam painted a picture of Sarah with her flying fingers.

And one of Flo holding the trophy she'd just won.

"It looks just like you, Flo," said Sarah.

Then Sam painted a picture of Eugene and his computer with all its zips and zaps.

Sam's family thought that being able to paint
was something special . . .

and so did Sam.